C900905050

D062603?

MYSTERY

BLACK BEARD

Gillian Cross

With illustrations by
Peter Cottrill

Barrington  Stoke

First published in 2014 in Great Britain by
Barrington Stoke Ltd
18 Walker Street, Edinburgh, EH3 7LP

www.barringtonstoke.co.uk

Text © 2014 Gillian Cross
Illustrations © 2014 Peter Cottrill

The moral right of Gillian Cross and Peter Cottrill to be
identified as the author and illustrator of this work has been
asserted in accordance with the Copyright, Designs and
Patents Act, 1988

All rights reserved. No part of this publication may be
reproduced in whole or in any part in any form without the
written permission of the publisher

A CIP catalogue record for this book is available
from the British Library upon request

ISBN: 978-1-78112-359-1

Printed in China by Leo

Contents

Chapter 1
Two Strange Men

Annie's dad solved crimes. A sign on his office door said –

Bill Clark
Crime Buster

Sometimes Annie's dad stayed at home and hunted for clues on the internet. Sometimes he went out to look for clues. Whatever he did, all his work was top secret – and lots of strange people came to see him in his office.

One Saturday afternoon, Annie was doing her English homework. She was trying to write a poem about bananas when there was a knock at the front door.

Bang! Bang! Bang!

"Who's that?" Annie's gran shouted from upstairs. "I'm in the bath!"

Annie went to open the door. There was a very tall man outside. He was as tall as Annie's dad and he was wearing a long black coat and a big black hat. Most of his face was hidden by a thick, curly beard.

The beard was as black as night.

"Um – hello," Annie said. "Do you want to see my dad?"

"Yes!" the man said. "Where is he?"

"I'll tell him you're here," said Annie. "What's your name?"

"Never mind that," said the man. "Just tell him he's got a visitor."

Annie went across the hall and knocked on her dad's office door. "Someone to see you," she called.

"Who is it?" her dad called back.

But before Annie could reply, the man with the black beard marched into the house. He opened the office door and went straight in.

'What a rude man!' Annie thought, as the man with the black beard slammed the door behind him. She went back into the sitting room and started thinking about her banana poem again.

But she had only just begun to write when there was another knock on the front door. This time it was very quiet.

Tap, tap, tap.

Annie opened the door again. There was another man outside. He was much shorter than the first one. He was wearing jeans and a T-shirt and he had bright yellow hair.

And no beard.

The man grinned at Annie. "Hi," he said. "My name's Jed. I've come to see your dad."

"I'll tell him you're here," Annie said.

"No need," said Jed. "He knows I'm coming."

Jed pushed past Annie and ran across the hall. As quick as a flash, he opened the office door, slipped inside and shut the door behind him.

'That's odd,' Annie thought. 'He's totally different from the other man – but his voice is the same. And he's just as rude.'

Annie went back into the sitting room, but before she could pick up her banana poem the office door opened again. Annie heard a very weird dragging sound. She ran into the hall to see what it was.

Jed was staggering out of the office and the man with the black beard was leaning on him.

"What's the matter?" Annie asked.

"He's ill," said Jed. "I have to take him home."

The man with the black beard was so floppy that Jed had to hold him up. Annie couldn't see whether he looked ill or not, because his face was hidden by the black hat and the black beard.

"Oh dear," she said. "Can I help?"

Jed nodded. "My van's outside," he said. "Go and open the back doors."

Annie ran out into the street. There was a small orange van parked by the kerb. She opened the back doors and Jed dragged the other man round to the back of the van.

"Now open the driver's door!" Jed snapped.

Annie ran round to the front of the van. There was a loud thump as Jed dumped the man with the black beard into the back of the van. Then Jed slammed the doors, came round to the front and pushed Annie out of the way. He jumped into the driver's seat and drove off at top speed.

'How rude!' Annie thought again. 'What's the big hurry?' Then it struck her that Jed might be taking the other man to hospital and she felt a bit bad.

Annie wanted to ask her dad about the two men, but when she knocked on his office door there was no reply. So she went back to her English poem. But it was VERY HARD to think about bananas. She kept watching the office in case her dad came out.

He didn't.

At 6 p.m., Gran came into the sitting room. "Tea will be ready in ten minutes," she said. "Tell your dad, Annie."

Annie knocked on her dad's office door. "Tea in ten minutes!" she yelled.

But her dad didn't come out.

Ten minutes later, she yelled again. "Tea's ready, Dad!"

Still no Dad.

"You'll have to go and get him," Gran said in a cross voice.

Annie went and banged on the office door. "It's tea time!" she shouted. She pushed the door open. "Come on, Dad!" she said.

But Dad wasn't there.

The office was empty.

Chapter 2
An Empty Room

Where was Dad?

'He can't have gone out,' Annie thought.
'I would have seen him. I was watching the
office door all the time.'

Annie looked under the desk. She looked
behind the curtains and in the cupboard. But Dad
wasn't hiding there. He wasn't in the office at all.

Annie went back to Gran at the dinner table. "Dad's not in his office," she said. "But he can't have gone out. I was watching the door."

"You must have missed him," Gran said. She was very cross now. "Stupid man! Why didn't he say he was going out? I'll have to keep his tea hot."

Gran picked up Dad's plate of chicken pie and took it back into the kitchen.

Annie began to eat. Gran made the best chicken pie in the world, but Annie didn't notice how good it was. She couldn't stop thinking about her dad's empty office. She knew she hadn't missed him. The office door had been shut all the time. So where was Dad?

Annie wolfed down the rest of her tea, then she went back to the office to try and work out what was going on. She had to find out if Dad was OK.

But she didn't know where to start. There were no papers on the desk. No messages on the notice board. And she couldn't look on the computer, because it was off – and she didn't know the password.

But Annie did find her dad's coat, hanging on the back of the door. And that's how she knew she was right. Dad hadn't gone out. It was cold outside. He wouldn't have left the house without his coat.

Then Annie saw something bright and shiny under the desk. She bent down for a closer look. It was Dad's phone!

Annie shuddered. Something was very wrong. Dad never went anywhere without his phone. She grabbed it and ran back to Gran.

"Look!" she said. "Dad's left his phone behind. Why would he do that? I think something bad has happened. I think Dad's in trouble."

"Nonsense!" said Gran. "He's just up to his usual tricks. He's like a little boy playing games. Why doesn't he get a proper job?" And she switched on the TV very loud, so she couldn't hear Annie's voice.

Annie didn't know what to do. She went back into the office and looked around. What had happened? Had Dad just – disappeared? That idea gave her a spooky feeling. She shivered, as if a cold wind was blowing on the back of her neck.

"Don't be silly," she said to herself. "You're making things up!"

But – wait a minute! Annie wasn't making things up. There was a cold wind blowing on the back of her neck! She ran across to the window and saw it wasn't shut properly.

That was odd. Dad NEVER opened the window. He said it was a waste of heat.

But the window was open now.

Annie opened it wider and leaned out.
There was a flower bed underneath the window
and when she looked down she saw marks in
the earth.

Footprints!

The two nearest ones were deeper than
the rest, as if someone had jumped out of the
window and landed heavily. Had Dad left the
room that way? Annie looked harder at the
footprints.

They weren't her dad's. His feet were
much bigger than that and he always wore old
trainers. These footprints were quite small.
And they looked as if they'd been made by
someone wearing boots.

'There's a mystery here,' Annie thought.
'And I have to solve it! But how?'

Annie knew she couldn't do it on her own. She took out her phone and texted her best friends, Matt and Ruth. The text said –

"Need your help. Please come now."

Chapter 3
Black Platform Boots

It took Matt and Ruth exactly seven minutes to get to Annie's house. Matt swooped up the road on his bike just as Ruth whizzed round the corner on hers.

Annie was watching out for them. She opened the front door before they had time to ring the bell.

"My dad's vanished," she whispered. "And there are footprints outside his office window. Come and see."

16

She took Ruth and Matt into the office and opened the window wide. "Look!" she said.

Matt and Ruth leaned out of the window.

"I can see that someone's jumped out of this window," Matt said. "How do you know it wasn't your dad?"

"His feet are much bigger than those footprints," said Annie.

"I want to take a closer look," said Ruth. "I'm going outside."

"Mind the footprints," said Annie. "They're the only clues we've got."

"I'll be careful," said Ruth. She climbed out of the window and jumped down into the flower bed. "Yuck!" she said as she landed.

"What's the matter?" asked Matt.

Ruth pulled a face. "I've got something sticky on my shoe," she said. "It looks like pink chewing gum."

She pulled a long gloop of pink gum off her shoe and threw it under a bush. But it didn't land on the ground.

It hit something black and shiny, half hidden under some leaves.

"Hey!" said Annie. "What's that?"

"Don't know," said Ruth. She bent down to reach under the bush. "Look what I've found!" she shouted.

She pulled out two black boots with thick platform soles.

"Wow! Another clue!" said Annie. "Do they match the footprints?"

Ruth turned the boots over to look at the soles. "Yuck, yuck!" she said. "More nasty pink gum."

"Never mind the gum," said Matt. "Do those boots match the footprints?"

Ruth put the boots down next to the footprints. "Yes, they do!" she said. "They're a perfect match. The person who jumped out of the office window was wearing these boots."

"It wasn't my dad," said Annie. "Those boots wouldn't fit on his great big feet."

"Who else has been in the office today?" Matt asked. "Did your dad have any visitors?"

Annie nodded. "Yes! Two strange men came to see him. The first one was very tall, with a big black hat and a black beard. And the second one was small, with yellow hair. He was called Jed."

Ruth took a deep breath. "Maybe there weren't really two men," she said. "Maybe there was only one man. The first time he came, he wore these boots with the platform soles. So he looked very tall. And he had a hat to hide his hair."

"And a fake beard," Matt said. "To hide his face."

"That's right!" said Ruth. "He went into the office and took off the hat and the beard. Then he jumped out of the window and hid his boots in that bush. And when he knocked on the front door again, you thought he was a different man. Because he looked much shorter and you could see his yellow hair."

"Brilliant!" said Matt. "We've solved the mystery!"

But Annie shook her head. "There were two men. They came out of the office together. Jed was dragging the man with the black beard."

"The man with the black beard must have been your dad," Ruth said. "Jed knocked him out – POW! BIFF! POW! – and then dressed him up in black clothes. With the hat and the beard to hide his face."

"But he didn't need the platform boots," said Matt. "Because your dad really is tall. So he jumped out of the window again to hide the boots in that bush."

"That must be what happened!" Ruth said.

Annie nodded. "You could be right," she said. "And I've just remembered something else. Those two men looked different – but their voices were exactly the same."

"You see!" said Ruth. "I knew I was right. There was only one man – with a plan to snatch your dad."

"So he took my dad away in his van?" said Annie. "You mean –"

Ruth nodded. "Yes. Your dad's been kidnapped!"

Chapter 4
The Notebook

Annie stared at Ruth. "But why?" she said. "Why would anyone want to kidnap my dad?"

"Your dad's a Crime Buster, isn't he?" said Matt. "Maybe he'd found out something bad about Jed. Perhaps Jed is a criminal. Perhaps Jed is a GANG BOSS!"

"Yes!" said Ruth. "That must be why Jed kidnapped him. To stop him going to the police."

"But what did Dad find out about Jed?" said Annie.

"We can't tell," said Matt. "Unless we look in his files."

"But all his files are on the computer," wailed Annie. "And I don't know the password."

Ruth frowned. "What does he use when he goes out looking for clues?" she said. "He must write things down then. He can't take his computer out with him."

"He's got a little notebook," Annie said. "He's always scribbling in that. 'No one can hack my notebook!' he says."

Matt grinned. "We need that notebook," he said. "Where is it?"

"It might be in his coat," said Annie. "Wait a minute." She took her dad's coat off the door and began to feel in the pockets.

There was nothing in the first pocket. Or in the second one. But when Annie slipped her hand into the inside pocket she felt something small and flat.

"It's here!" she said. She pulled out the notebook and opened it. Matt and Ruth came to look over her shoulder.

A newspaper cutting was stuck on the first page of the notebook. It said –

Another Mystery Bank Robbery

When the staff of the Grand Central Bank arrived for work this morning, they found the strong room door open and the strong room empty. All the money had disappeared.

"Another robbery!" said the bank manager. "You need seven different keys to open our strong room. How did the robber copy all those?"

This is the fifth bank robbery this month.

"We are baffled," said Police Officer Peel. "We do not have a single clue to follow."

"Dad must be working on those robberies," Annie said. "I wonder what he's found out."

She turned to the next page to look for more notes. An address was scribbled at the top of the page –

17 Brook Lane

Below that was a single word, written in red and underlined three times –

<u>**Bubbles**</u>

All the other pages in the notebook were blank.

"What does 'Bubbles' mean?" said Matt. "You can't rob a bank with bubbles."

"It doesn't make sense," said Annie. "I think we should call the police."

"Let's go and ask your gran to phone them," said Ruth.

Gran was still watching TV at full volume in the sitting room. Annie tried to tell her about the clues they'd found, but when they showed her the boots and the notebook she just laughed.

"Oh, Annie," she said. "You're just like your dad. Always playing daft games."

"It's not a game!" said Annie. "It's real. I want to ring the police."

Gran stopped laughing. "Don't you dare!" she said. "I've told you – your dad's bound to be OK. He'll be furious if you get mixed up with his work. Stay away from the police."

"But Gran –" Annie said.

Gran frowned at her. "That's enough," she said. "Stop bothering me with your silly stories." And with that, Gran turned her back on Annie and started watching TV again.

Annie went back into the office with her two friends, feeling gloomy. "It's no good," she said. "We can't call the police now. Gran will just tell them we're playing games."

"So what can we do?" said Ruth. "Do we have to give up?"

"No!" Annie shouted. "We can't do that. My dad's been kidnapped. We've got to rescue him."

"But how can we?" asked Matt. "Your gran's a grown-up. We're only kids."

Annie opened her dad's notebook again. "We've got the address Dad wrote in here," she said. "Look – 17 Brook Lane. Let's go there. See what we can find out."

"What? Now?" said Ruth.

"Of course," said Annie. "There's no time to waste. We've got to find Dad!"

Chapter 5
Brook Lane

Annie found a map in her dad's office. They looked at it to see where Brook Lane was. It was right over on the other side of town.

"That's MILES away!" said Matt. "It'll take us ages to get there."

"Not if we go on our bikes," said Annie. "We can be there in half an hour. Come on."

She went to the shed to get her bike and they set off as fast as they could.

"Keep your eyes open for clues!" Annie called. "We might see some on the way."

They hadn't even reached the corner of the road when Ruth stopped.

"Yuck!" she said.

"What's the matter?" said Matt. "Is it a clue?"

Ruth shook her head. "No, it's some more of that horrible pink gum. It's stuck on my wheel."

"Don't fuss," said Annie. "We've got to get to 17 Brook Lane as fast as we can!"

They whizzed on round the corner and down the main road. They kept cycling over blobs of pink gum. Some of it stuck to Annie's front wheel and she had to pedal harder, to stop the wheel sticking to the road. But she didn't stop. She was in too much of a hurry.

By the time they reached Brook Lane, they were all out of breath. But Annie wouldn't let them rest.

"Come on!" she said. "Let's find number 17. I bet there's an orange van parked outside. That's Jed's van – I'm sure it'll be there."

But the van wasn't there. The road outside number 17 was empty.

"Let's see if the van's in the garage," Ruth said.

"The garage door isn't quite shut," said Matt. "I'm going to look inside. Hold my bike."

"Be careful!" said Ruth. "What if Jed sees you?"

"He won't," said Matt. "Look! I'll hide behind that hedge."

Matt crouched down and started creeping along behind the hedge. Annie felt her heart thudding in her chest. Suppose Jed was in the garage? What then?

When Matt reached the garage, he crept out from behind the hedge. He walked up to the garage door on tiptoes and peeped inside. Ruth and Annie saw him shake his head. Then he sneaked back along the hedge to Ruth and Annie.

"There's nothing in the garage," Matt told them. "And the house looks empty. I think we're too late."

"We can't just go away," Annie said. "Number 17 Brook Lane is the only clue we've got to help us find Dad. I'm going to knock on the front door."

"No!" Ruth hissed. "It could be dangerous!"

But Annie didn't care about danger. She needed to rescue her dad. She marched up to the front of the house and peered in at the windows. It looked as if Matt was right. All the rooms were empty. She banged on the door anyway, just in case someone was inside.

"It's no good knocking," shouted a voice behind her. "He's gone."

Annie turned round and saw a girl in running kit coming out of the house across the road.

"There's no one at number 17," the girl called. "The man who lived there moved out. He came and collected his last few things about an hour ago."

"Who was he?" Matt asked. "Who lived here?"

The girl jogged across the road. "I never knew his name," she said. "He didn't talk to anyone else in the street."

"Well – what did he look like?" Annie asked. "Did he have yellow hair? And an orange van?"

The girl nodded. "Disgusting man!" she said. "He made me sick, dropping his horrible sticky bubble gum everywhere."

Annie stared at her. "Dropping his – what?" she said.

"His bubble gum," said the girl. She pointed at the pink blobs on the road. "Disgusting stuff! He drops it everywhere he goes. It gets all over my trainers. Yuck!"

Annie looked at Ruth and Matt.

Ruth and Matt looked at Annie.

"It's not chewing gum that's sticking on our bikes," said Ruth. "It's –"

"Bubble gum!!!" they all yelled together.

That was why Annie's dad had written "Bubbles" in his notebook. The bank robber must have left blobs of bubble gum behind when he robbed the banks.

So that must mean that Jed was the bank robber.

"Now we can find him," shouted Annie. "All we have to do is follow the trail of pink gum!"

"Thank you," Ruth said to the girl. "Thank you, thank you, thank you!"

"Just find him," the girl said. "If you can get rid of his nasty gum, you'll make this town a better place for runners."

Ruth, Matt and Annie all jumped on their bikes and raced up Brook Lane as fast as they could pedal.

Chapter 6
On the Trail

There was a line of pink blobs all up the middle of the road. It was easy to follow the pink blobs, but not so easy not to cycle over them.

When the friends reached the crossroads, Matt looked both ways and gave a shout.

"We need to turn right," he said. "I can see the blobs going that way!"

"Can we stop a minute?" Ruth wailed. "I want to get the gum off my wheels."

"No time!" Annie shouted. "We've got to find my dad!"

Annie had lots of bubble gum on her wheels too. But she knew they had to keep going. They had to find that orange van.

The bubble gum trail led them past shops and houses and out onto the very edge of town. Soon they found themselves in a place full of old, empty factories. The factories were grey and dirty with lots of broken windows.

"I'm scared," Ruth said. "This is a horrible place. Let's go back."

Annie was scared too, but she could see more pink blobs ahead of them. "Let's go round the next corner," she whispered. "But be quiet. If Jed is here we don't want him to hear us coming."

They got off their bikes and pushed them up to the corner. Annie peered round.

There was the orange van!

It was a little way up the road, parked outside a dark old factory. The back doors of the van were wide open and there was nothing inside.

"Jed must have taken my dad into that factory," Annie whispered. "I'm going to see if I can see anything through the window."

Ruth shivered. "Don't let Jed spot you," she whispered back. "Be careful."

Annie nodded. Inch by inch, she crept forward until she was right outside the factory. She stood flat against the wall, bent her head to the side and peeped in at the window.

And there was her dad.

He was sitting on a chair in the middle of a big empty room. There were ropes round his arms and legs, tying him to the chair. And he had a gag in his mouth, so he couldn't speak. But his eyes were open.

His eyes were on Jed.

Jed was on the other side of the room, standing by a long table. Annie could see a row of pink blobs on the table. They looked like blobs of bubble gum.

But why would Jed put bubble gum blobs in a row on the table? Annie pressed her ear close to the window to try and hear what he was saying.

"Want to know how I robbed those banks?" Jed said to Annie's dad. "I bet you can't guess!" He laughed a horrible laugh.

Annie's dad couldn't say anything. He just kept staring at Jed.

"I couldn't steal all five sets of keys at once, could I?" Jed said. And he laughed again.

Annie saw her dad look across at the bubble gum on the table. Then he looked back at Jed.

"That's right!" Jed said. "I stole the keys at different times – and copied them. Clever, eh? I pressed the keys into bits of bubble gum. Then I used those bubble gum shapes to make new keys. And you didn't guess, did you, Mr Crime Buster?"

Annie's dad growled behind his gag.

Jed gave a nasty grin. "And now I'm ready for my last – and biggest – robbery," he said. "And you won't be able to stop me. I've already made the keys I need."

Jed picked a big bunch of keys off the table and jangled them. He had an even nastier grin on his face now. "Know what I'm going to do with these?" he jeered.

Annie's dad shook his head and growled again.

Jed gave an evil chuckle. "I'm going to break into the Crown City Bank and steal twelve billion pounds!"

Annie's dad shook his head angrily and pulled at the ropes that tied his arms. He tried and tried, but he couldn't break free.

Jed laughed out loud. "I'll be rich," he gloated. "And famous! But no one will know who I am. And you'll never tell them – because you're going to disappear."

'No!' thought Annie. 'No!' What was Jed going to do now?

Annie watched in horror as Jed reached for a long handle on the floor and pulled it down. "Goodbye, for ever!" he yelled. "I win and you lose, Mr Crime Buster!"

There was a loud creaking sound and Annie saw a trap door open under her dad's chair.

The chair fell through the hole, with Annie's dad still tied to it.

"No one will ever find you!" Jed shouted into the hole. He slammed the trap door shut.

The trap door fitted into the floor so well that Annie could hardly see where it was – except for one little keyhole. Jed took an old black key off the table and pushed it into the keyhole. He locked the trap door and then, with another horrible chuckle, he dropped the key into his pocket.

Annie's dad was a prisoner under the floor.

The key was in Jed's pocket.

Without the key, how could Annie get her dad out?

Chapter 7
Stop Him!

Very, very carefully, Annie crept away from the factory wall. She tiptoed back to Matt and Ruth as fast as she could.

"We have to call the police!" she whispered. "My dad's a prisoner under the floor in that factory. And Jed is planning a really big bank robbery."

Matt took out his phone. "Use this," he said.

Annie tapped 999 into the phone.

"Emergency services," a voice said. "Which service do you need? Fire? Ambulance? Police?"

"Police!" Annie said. "As fast as you can!"

"I'm connecting you now," said the voice.

In two seconds, Annie was talking to a policewoman. "My dad's been taken prisoner," she told her. "He's in one of the broken-down factories on the edge of town."

"Which factory?" the policewoman asked.

Annie looked round. "It has 'The Best Wash' painted on the front."

"That's the old washing machine factory," the policewoman said. "We'll come straight away."

"Please hurry!" said Annie. "My dad's in danger."

"Ten minutes," the policewoman said. "Sit tight."

Annie gave the phone back to Matt. "I hope they hurry," she said. "I want to get my dad out of there fast."

"Let's watch the factory," said Matt. "To make sure Jed doesn't get away."

They crouched down behind a low wall. Annie and Matt watched the factory, and Ruth started pulling bubble gum off their bikes.

"Nasty sticky stuff," she muttered. "Look how much there is!" She rolled it all up into one lump. "It's as big as a football!" she said. "I need a bin to put it in."

"Not now," said Annie. "We have to watch the factory."

Matt pointed across at it. "Look!" he whispered.

A man was walking out from behind the factory. He was very fat and he had a big messy mop of grey hair.

"Who's that?" Annie said.

"I've never seen him before," said Matt.

The man walked up and down the road, checking if anyone was there. He didn't see Annie and Matt and Ruth behind the wall. When he reached the orange van, he shut the back doors. Then he opened the driver's door and got in.

"Oh no," said Ruth. "It must be Jed – in a wig and a fat suit."

"Stop him!" said Annie. "We can't let him get away!"

She started to stand up, but Matt and Ruth pulled her down again.

"Don't be silly!" Matt hissed. "Jed knows who you are. If he sees you, he might try to kidnap you too."

"But we must stop him," Annie said. "My dad's locked under the floor and Jed's got the key. What can we do?"

"Wait for the police to get here," said Matt. "We can't do anything by ourselves."

"Oh yes we can," said Ruth.

Matt and Annie looked at her in surprise and she gave them a big grin.

"I've just had a fantastic idea!" she said.

Chapter 8
Bubble!

"We can use this to stop Jed," Ruth said. She picked up the huge ball of bubble gum and took the pump off her bike. She pushed the end of the pump into the bubble gum. "Quick!" she said. "Get your pumps too."

Annie watched in amazement as Ruth began to pump as hard as she could. The big ball of bubble gum got bigger and bigger and bigger.

"Brilliant!" said Matt.

He and Annie grabbed their pumps and pushed the ends into the bubble gum. With three of them pumping, the gum swelled up even faster. It turned into a huge bubble.

As big as a bike ...

Then as big as a car ...

Then as big as a bus!

And then they heard the orange van starting up.

"Quick!" Annie yelled. "Roll the bubble into the road!"

They heaved the big pink bubble over the wall. Using all their strength, they gave it an enormous push. SHLOOP! SHLOOP! SHLOOP! The horrible sticky bubble rolled out into the middle of the road just as the orange van started moving.

And the fat man with the messy grey hair – who was, of course, Jed – drove straight into the bubble.

Splat!

The orange van disappeared into the pink gum. There was gum all over the windscreen. All over the doors. All over the wheels. The van was one huge, sticky, pink lump.

And that was when the children heard the sirens of the police cars.

Nee-naw! Nee-naw! Nee-naw!

"Hurray!" yelled Ruth. "Just in time."

Jed heard the police cars too. He pushed the van door open and tried to fight his way out of the sticky pink bubble. But the gum was too strong. It covered him as well as the van and he couldn't struggle free. He was still struggling when two police cars raced round

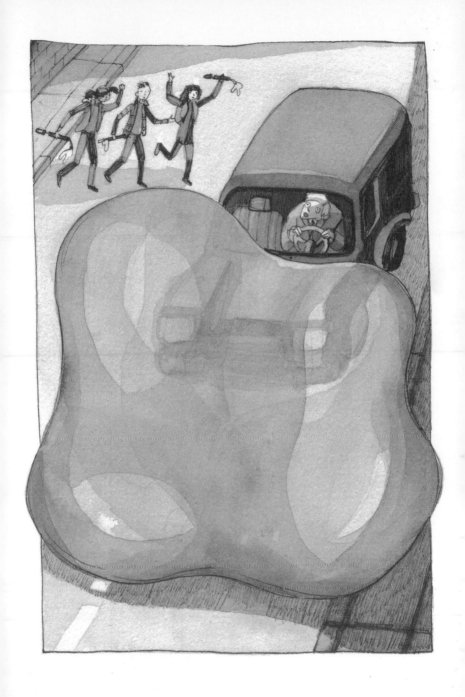

the corner. They pulled up, one on each side of the van, and lots of police officers jumped out.

"What's going on?" said a policeman.

Annie ran out from behind the wall. "We've caught the bank robber!" she shouted. "Look in his pockets!"

The police officers pulled Jed out from the sticky pink bubbly mess and put handcuffs on him. Then they searched his pockets. They found the keys he'd made to break into the Crown City Bank. And they found another key too. An old black key.

"That's the key I need," said Annie. "I have to unlock my dad!"

Annie snatched the key and ran into the factory. Matt and Ruth ran after her and two of the police officers followed them.

When they got into the factory, the police officers looked puzzled. "How can your dad be in here?" one of them said. "There's nowhere to hide."

"Oh yes there is," said Annie. She bent down and put the black key into the keyhole in the floor. "You'll have to move," she said to the police officers. "You're on top of the trap door."

The police officers jumped out of the way and Annie turned the key. There was the same loud creaking noise as before and the trap door fell open.

"My dad's down there," Annie said.

One of the police officers jumped down into the hole and lifted up the chair – with Annie's dad still tied to it. The other police officer heaved the chair onto the factory floor, away from the trap door.

Annie rushed to her dad and undid the gag around his mouth.

"Are you OK, Dad?" she asked.

"Yes," said her dad. "But never mind that – I know who's robbing all those banks. We have to go after him!"

"It's OK," said Matt. "We've got him."

"Look!" said Annie.

She opened the factory door so they could see into the road. Police officers were pulling bubble gum off Jed and the messy grey wig had come off with it. They could all see Jed's bright yellow hair.

Annie's dad was amazed. "However did you do it?" he said.

"It was nothing." Annie shrugged. "We just needed a few clues," she said with a grin. "And an amazing giant bubble gum trap!"

Our books are tested
for children and young people by
children and young people.

Thanks to everyone who consulted on
a manuscript for their time and effort in
helping us to make our books better
for our readers.